Y0-BDI-861

# Too Much
## of a Good Thing

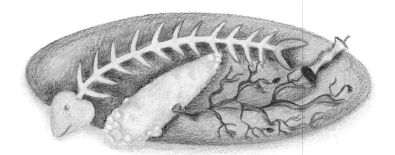

Mira Wasserman
*illustrated by*
Christine Mannone Carolan

KAR-BEN
PUBLISHING

*For my two Shabbat boys, Yosef Gavriel and Hillel Adar.*
*—M.W.*

*Havdalah* (literally "separation"), is recited over a cup of wine at the end of the Sabbath and holidays to emphasize the distinction between the sacred and the ordinary. The Havdalah service is among the most ancient. It is said to have been instituted by the "Men of the Great Synagogue" during the time of the Second Temple, and versions of the blessings appear in the *Jerusalem Talmud*.

The story of Antoninus's Shabbat visit to Rabbi Judah the Prince appears in the *Babylonian Talmud (Shabbat 119a)* and in *Genesis Rabbah (11:4)*.

Text copyright © 2004 by Mira Wasserman
Illustrations copyright © 2004 by Christine Mannone Carolan

All rights reserved. International copyright secured. No part of this book may be reproduced, stored in a retrieval system, or transmitted in any form or by any means—electronic, mechanical, photocopying, recording, or otherwise—without the prior written permission of Lerner Publications Company, except for the inclusion of brief quotations in an acknowledged review.

KAR-BEN PUBLISHING, INC.
A division of Lerner Publishing Group
241 First Avenue North
Minneapolis, MN 55401 U.S.A.
800–4KARBEN

Website address: www.karben.com

Library of Congress Cataloging-in-Publication Data

Wasserman, Mira
    Too much of a good thing / by Mira Wasserman ; illustrated by Christine Carolan.
        p.    cm.
    Summary: After learning about Shabbat from his friend, Rabbi Judah, a Roman king decrees a bigger, better Shabbat in his kingdom, and the rabbi must come to teach him what truly makes Shabbat sweet.
    ISBN: 1–58013–082–8 (lib. bdg. : alk. paper)
    ISBN: 1–58013–066–6 (pbk. : alk. paper)
    [1. Sabbath—Fiction. 2. Judaism—Customs and Practices—Fiction. 3. Kings, queens, rulers, etc.—Fiction. 4. Rabbis—Fiction. 5. Jews—Fiction.] I. Carolan, Christine, ill. II. Title.
PZ7.W25863 To 2003
[Fic]—dc21                                              2002152167

Manufactured in the United States of America
1 2 3 4 5 6 – JR – 09 08 07 06 05 04

**L**ong, long ago in the Land of Israel, there lived a great Jewish teacher called Rabbi Judah, who was friends with a Roman king named Antoninus, the ruler of a neighboring province.

Like other Romans, Antoninus liked things BIG and impressive. He liked a BIG palace, a BIG meal, and a BIG nap. He especially liked BIG ideas.

King Antoninus enjoyed visiting his Jewish friend, and each time he came, he hoped that the rabbi would have something BIG to teach him.

But on each visit, the king would remark upon how small the rabbi's house was, how small the Land of Israel was, and how small were all the matters the rabbi cared about.

Rabbi Judah spent most of his time with other rabbis discussing things like how to pray, how to celebrate holidays, and how to help the poor. King Antoninus was interested in BIGGER things — how to collect more taxes, how to build more roads, and how to conquer new territory.

One Saturday, King Antoninus paid a visit to Rabbi Judah.   He was amazed to see how humble a meal the family was eating — stew, cold vegetables, some braided bread, and wine.   This is what Rabbi Judah proposed to serve a Roman King?  Antoninus was so insulted, he turned on his heels to go.

Rabbi Judah welcomed the king warmly.  "Please join me, my friend, for our Shabbat meal.  It is a small and simple meal — our laws of Shabbat forbid us from cooking today — but  I don't think you'll be disappointed."

King Antoninus sat down with the rabbi's family. They recited blessings over the wine and braided bread and began to eat. The meal, though simple, was the most delicious the king had ever tasted. After every bowl was licked clean, and every crumb was eaten, the family prayed and sang.

King Antoninus proclaimed, "I've never eaten such a wonderful meal."

"You're welcome anytime, King Antoninus," the rabbi offered. "Why don't you come next Shabbat?"

"Oh, I don't think I can wait that long for such tasty morsels. I'll be here on Tuesday," the king answered.

When Antoninus arrived on Tuesday, he was pleased to see that Rabbi Judah had prepared a feast truly fit for a king. The table was laden with every kind of meat, rich soups, breads, cakes, and pies. Antoninus could barely wait for the blessing so that he could dig in.

He sampled a bit of every-thing — the meat was tender, the bread fresh from the oven — but something was missing.

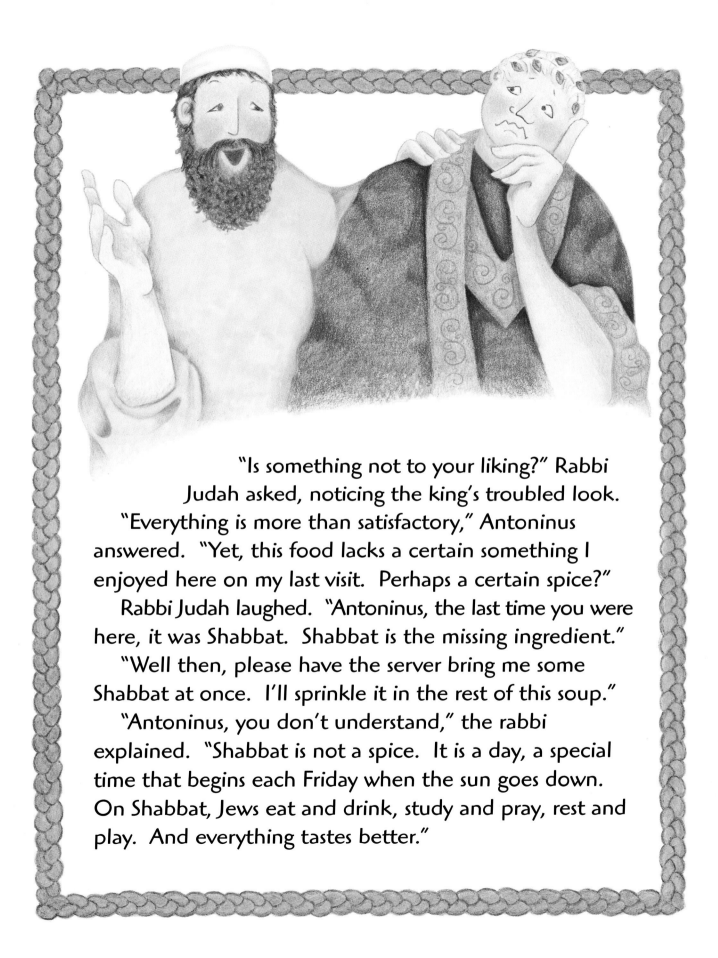

"Is something not to your liking?" Rabbi Judah asked, noticing the king's troubled look.

"Everything is more than satisfactory," Antoninus answered. "Yet, this food lacks a certain something I enjoyed here on my last visit. Perhaps a certain spice?"

Rabbi Judah laughed. "Antoninus, the last time you were here, it was Shabbat. Shabbat is the missing ingredient."

"Well then, please have the server bring me some Shabbat at once. I'll sprinkle it in the rest of this soup."

"Antoninus, you don't understand," the rabbi explained. "Shabbat is not a spice. It is a day, a special time that begins each Friday when the sun goes down. On Shabbat, Jews eat and drink, study and pray, rest and play. And everything tastes better."

"Shabbat sounds wonderful. I would like to have some myself, if you'll teach me how."

Rabbi Judah taught Antoninus the laws of Shabbat: how on Shabbat, everyone — kings and servants, peddlers and farmers, grownups and children, cows and horses — must rest. No planting or plowing, no buying or selling, no cooking or lighting fires.

King Antoninus thanked Rabbi Judah and set off for home so he could teach his own people the joys of Shabbat.

As he made his way, King Antoninus had a thought. The Jews enjoyed Shabbat for just one day each week. Antoninus would make Shabbat even better, even BIGGER. He would proclaim that in HIS province, Shabbat would last the whole week long.

When Antoninus arrived home, he issued a proclamation. "From now on, kings and servants, peddlers and farmers, grownups and children, cows and horses must rest. No 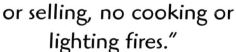 planting or plowing, no buying or selling, no cooking or lighting fires."

At first all the people
celebrated. The peddlers dropped
their heavy packs, the farmers
set down their hoes, the boys
and girls danced around singing,
"On Shabbat we
eat and drink,
study and pray, rest
and play...and everything tastes better."
    For the next week, families spent long
hours around the table eating, drinking,
singing, and talking.  They took long
afternoon naps, and enjoyed their
evenings visiting with friends.

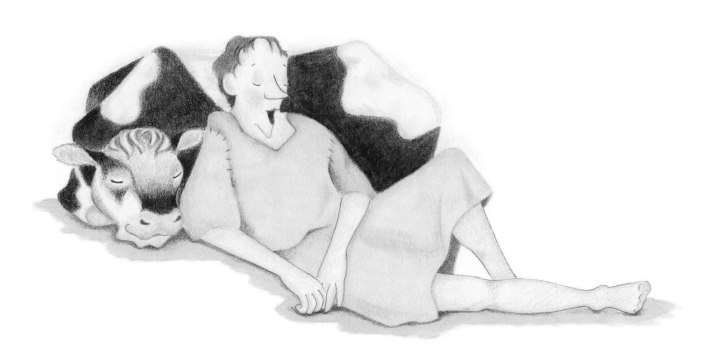

Soon though, things started to change. The villagers noticed it first. They were coming to the end of the food they had stored away, and since it was Shabbat they couldn't pick more vegetables from the garden, or bake more loaves of bread, or harvest grapes to make new wine. They began to get hungry.

It didn't take long until the palace cupboard was bare as well. Antoninus ordered his cook to go out and buy more provisions, but then he remembered: no buying or selling on Shabbat, and no cooking.

The situation got more serious as the days of Shabbat wore on.  Garbage piled up in the streets and wild animals descended on the fields, eating up all the crops the farmers had left unpicked.  People tried to go on praying and singing, but with no food to eat, Shabbat was not very much fun.

To make matters worse, the last fires in the province burned out.  The people shivered, their stomachs groaned, and they began to get restless.

The king was confused.  He thought Shabbat was the greatest idea he'd ever had, and yet it didn't seem to be working out.  He buried himself under his blankets to fend off the cold, and to hide from his people who gathered outside the palace calling on the king to get them food and fire.

Back in the Land of Israel, Rabbi Judah heard about the suffering in Antoninus's province and realized that something was very wrong. He had to let the king know that as sweet as Shabbat was, it needed the other days of the week for working, planting, buying, and selling.

Rabbi Judah gathered three items: a bottle of wine, a braided candle, and a box full of spices. With these supplies, he was sure he could convince King Antoninus to end Shabbat.

The rabbi traveled three days to get to Antoninus's province. He arrived in the dark of night, and used the flame of the braided candle to light his way to the palace. He knocked on the door.

A guard fumbled in the dark to open the door. "A flame," he cried out when he saw Rabbi Judah. "We haven't had any fire in this province for days and days!"

Rabbi Judah smiled. "I'd like to see King Antoninus," he said.

The guard remembered Antoninus's orders. "No one may see the king," he announced.

"In that case," said the rabbi, "perhaps I can visit with you. Would you care for some wine?"

The guard had not seen wine for some time.

Rabbi Judah recited a blessing and poured the guard one cup, and then another, and another. The guard gulped them down, and soon he became very sleepy.

"Excuse me, Rabbi, while I close my eyes..." the guard said, as he sank to the floor, snoring.

Still carrying the candle, Rabbi Judah entered the palace. He found the king in his bed shivering.

"Rabbi," Antoninus exclaimed. "It has been days since I've seen a flame, and longer since I've had anything to eat. I'm having second thoughts about this Shabbat of yours." With that, the king burst into the biggest sobs the rabbi had ever seen.

"There, there," said Rabbi Judah. "I've come to tell you that a Shabbat that never ends is too much of a good thing. It is time for your people to say goodbye to Shabbat and get back to work."

Antoninus said, "I would love to tell my people that Shabbat is over, but when I think of all the work that needs to be done, I get so tired, all I can do is hide." He sobbed some more.

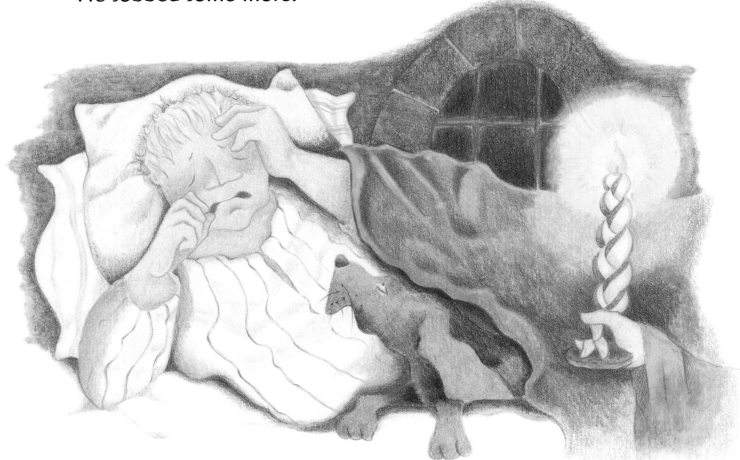

Rabbi Judah pulled the spices from his pocket and waved them under Antoninus's nose. The king drew in a long breath and stopped crying.

"These spices remind me of the sweetness of Shabbat at your house," Antoninus said.

The rabbi nodded. "Our Shabbat is sweet because we say goodbye to it each week. And we know that no matter how hard we work during the week, Shabbat always comes back again."

In the morning, when the sun rose and the angry crowds once again gathered outside the palace, King Antoninus and Rabbi Judah went out to meet them. "It is time to say goodbye to Shabbat and go back to work," Antoninus proclaimed. "But don't worry, soon we'll have a chance to rest again. From now on, there will be six days of work and one day of Shabbat each week."

Rabbi Judah taught all the people how to say goodbye to Shabbat. "The ceremony is called Havdalah," he explained. "Havdalah means to separate. We recite blessings over a braided candle, sweet-smelling spices, and a cup of wine, and announce that Shabbat has ended, and a new week has begun."

So King Antonius recited Havdalah and sent his people back to work.

Rabbi Judah made his way through the province to return home. He passed peddlers carrying packs, farmers gathering crops, and boys and girls baking bread.

"We'd like to sit and chat with you, Rabbi," they said, "but we have lots of work to do before Shabbat."

# HAVDALAH

*Light the havdalah candle and raise the cup of wine:*

בָּרוּךְ אַתָּה יְיָ אֱלֹהֵֽינוּ מֶֽלֶךְ הָעוֹלָם, בּוֹרֵא פְּרִי הַגָּֽפֶן.

*Baruch Atah Adonai Eloheinu Melech ha'olam, borei p'ri hagafen.*

**Blessed are You, O God, for creating wine, a symbol of joy.**

*Raise the spice box:*

בָּרוּךְ אַתָּה יְיָ אֱלֹהֵֽינוּ מֶֽלֶךְ הָעוֹלָם, בּוֹרֵא מִינֵי בְשָׂמִים.

*Baruch Atah Adonai Eloheinu Melech ha'olam, borei minei v'samim.*

**Blessed are You, O God, for creating many fragrant spices.**

*Pass around the spice box so everyone can smell the spices.*

*Raise the candle:*

בָּרוּךְ אַתָּה יְיָ אֱלֹהֵֽינוּ מֶֽלֶךְ הָעוֹלָם, בּוֹרֵא מְאוֹרֵי הָאֵשׁ.

*Baruch Atah Adonai Eloheinu Melech ha'olam, borei m'orei ha'esh.*

**Blessed are You, O God, for the blessing of fire.**
**May it bring warmth and light to the world.**

*Hold hands toward the candlelight to see the shadows.*

בָּרוּךְ אַתָּה יְיָ הַמַּבְדִּיל בֵּין קוֹדֶשׁ לְחוֹל.

*Baruch Atah Adonai hamavdil bein kodesh l'chol.*

**Blessed are You, O God, for making the holy different from the everyday.**

*Pass the wine around and give everyone a sip.*
*Pour a few drops in a plate and use it to put out the candle.*

Shabbat has now ended; a new week begins.
May the days ahead be filled with the
blessings of health, life, and peace, and may
we come together next week to welcome
another Shabbat.

SHAVUAH TOV! A GOOD WEEK!

## About the Author/Illustrator

**Mira Wasserman** has been rabbi of Congregation Beth Shalom in Bloomington, IN since her ordination from Hebrew Union College in 1998. She enjoys studying and teaching the stories of the ancient rabbis and creating some of her own. She and her husband, Steve Weitzman, have two sons, Yosef Gavriel and Hillel Adar. This is Mira's first book.

**Christine Mannone Carolan,** a graduate of SUNY Stony Brook, taught and raised a family before returning to Pratt Institute and graduating with a degree in illustration. She is a quilter and paints custom canvas floor cloths. She, her husband, four children, and yellow lab live in Setauket, NY. This is Christine's first book.